TILLY

Nimrod
the
circus pony

Look out for the other books in the
Tilly's Pony Tails *series*

Magic Spirit
Red Admiral
Rosie
Samson
Lucky Chance
Solo
Pride and Joy
Neptune
Parkview Pickle
Nimrod
Moonshadow
Autumn Glory
Goliath

TILLY'S PONY TAILS

Nimrod
the
circus pony

PIPPA FUNNELL

Illustrated by Jennifer Miles

Orion
Children's Books

First published in Great Britain in 2010
by Orion Children's Books
a division of the Orion Publishing Group Ltd
Orion House
5 Upper St Martin's Lane
London WC2H 9EA
An Hachette UK Company

3 5 7 9 8 6 4 2

A catalogue record for this book is available from the British Library.

ISBN 978 1 4440 0090 0

Printed and bound in the UK by CPI Mackays, Chatham ME5 8TD

www.orionbooks.co.uk
www.tillysponytails.co.uk

*For Viceroy,
the inspiration behind the bracelet*

One

Tilly Redbrow loved anything and
everything to do with horses. She spent
every spare minute at Silver Shoe Farm,
where her dream horse, Magic Spirit, was
stabled. Tilly and Magic had a special bond.
Angela, Silver Shoe's owner, said it was
rare to see such a natural affinity between
a horse and a rider. Her father, Jack Fisher,
was sure that one day Tilly and Magic
would achieve amazing things together.

Tilly and Magic had joined Silver Shoe after Tilly helped to rescue him from a busy roadside in the town. Back then, Magic had been malnourished and neglected, and though Tilly had always adored horses, she'd never had the chance to ride. Now they were transformed. Magic was a stunning 16hh grey with top class potential.

And Tilly was a dedicated and talented rider.

This was how, on a wintery day, Tilly came to be riding Magic Spirit through one of the local countryside tracks, with her friends, Mia and Cally. Mia, who still hadn't got a horse of her own since growing out of her pony, Rosie, was exercising one of the riding school horses – a chestnut called Watson. Cally was on her dun Connemara, Mr Fudge.

They were working on their paces, getting their horses to trot and canter. Magic was wearing a new bit and was very responsive to Tilly's commands. She had to make sure her hands stayed relaxed, as he seemed to notice every tiny bit of tension.

'Watch out for that signpost up ahead,' warned Cally, as they turned the corner on to Cobbin's End Lane. 'That wasn't there a few weeks ago.'

Tilly looked up and saw a large rectangular sign staked into the ground. She knew unexpected or unfamiliar objects could sometimes spook horses, so she made sure Magic walked calmly, by nudging him gently with her heel and reassuring him in a soft voice. Even though she understood him well, his difficult past meant he could be cautious.

Luckily, neither Magic, Watson nor Mr Fudge seemed bothered by the sign. As they passed it, the girls took a closer look. It showed silhouettes of clowns, trapeze artists and performing horses, against a bright candy-striped background.

'Lyons' Circus Has Arrived,' read Tilly. 'Cool. We should go and see it.'

'Oh no,' said Mia. 'We're probably too late. Look what it says . . .'

Someone had stuck a sticker across the bottom: 'Last ever show tonight. Don't miss out!'

'Shame,' said Tilly. 'That sticker could be days old. I would've liked to have seen their horses. Never mind. I suppose there's always next year.'

'Doesn't sound like there'll *be* a next year,' said Cally. 'Last ever show. It must be closing down.'

Disappointed, the girls rode on. Tilly thought of the horses she'd seen at a circus when she was little. Beautiful Palominos, flying round the ring, with flowing manes and plumes of feathers attached to their saddles. She was disappointed she'd missed the chance to see more of them.

Suddenly through the trees, in the

large field beyond, she caught a glimpse of colour. Red and yellow stripes.

'What's that?' she whispered, slowing so as not to alarm Magic. Cally and Mia slowed with her.

'Looks like a tent,' said Cally.

'Not just a tent,' said Mia. 'That's the Big Top! Which means the circus is still in town!'

Tilly gasped. Magic felt the tension in her muscles and began to side-step, as though he was excited too.

'What do you think?' said Tilly, patting his neck. 'Shall we go to the circus and see those clever performing horses? I wish you could see them too. Maybe they could teach you a few tricks!'

Magic stamped his front hoof.

'Let's go tonight,' said Mia. 'Last chance ever, remember?'

'Good idea,' said Tilly. 'I'll check with my mum. We could make it a Silver Shoe Farm outing!'

'Plus me,' said Cally. 'I can be an honorary member, can't I?'

Cally had shared Rosie at Silver Shoe Farm with Mia, until her parents had moved to Dubai, and Tilly had taken over. Now Cally went to Cavendish Hall, the local boarding school where Tilly's brother, Brook, also attended. Cally visited Silver Shoe as often as she could because, like Tilly and Mia, it was the place she felt happiest.

'Do you think they'll have acrobats? And performing dogs? And people on stilts? I love the circus!' said Mia gleefully.

The girls turned their horses round and headed back towards the stables. They talked for the entire journey, non-stop chatter about Lyons' performing horses.

'What tricks do you think they do?' asked Tilly.

'Amazing stuff,' said Mia. 'I once saw a circus horse jump through a flaming hoop!'

'I bet they have fancy bridles,' said Cally. 'I can't wait to see them.'

Two

That evening, Tilly, her parents and her
younger brother, Adam, took their seats in
the Big Top. When Tilly had asked about
the circus, they'd all wanted to come. Next
to them sat Cally, Mia,
and Mia's parents, and
on the other side were
Angela and Duncan.
They shared bags of
toffee popcorn and
candy floss while they

waited for the show to begin. It was a packed audience.

Tilly loved the atmosphere. There was excitement in the air, which reminded her of her visit to the Olympia Horse Show last year. She could smell sawdust and manure, so she was certain she was going to see some horses tonight.

Suddenly the lights went down and a spotlight fell on the centre of the ring. Everyone hushed as a moustached man wearing a red tail coat and top hat appeared.

'Who's that?' said Adam. He'd never been to a circus before and was amazed by it all.

'That's the ringmaster,' said Tilly's dad. 'He's in charge.'

'Ladies and Gentlemen, welcome to Lyons' Circus!' said the ringmaster. His voice was loud and booming.

'It's a sad occasion and a happy occasion. It's sad because it is our last performance ever . . .'

The audience booed.

'And it's happy because it's going to be our BEST performance ever!'

Now, they cheered.

'So without further ado, I give you THE LYONS' CIRCUS!'

The ringmaster gestured towards the back of the tent. A small doorway opened and out came performers of all shapes and sizes: clowns, jugglers, tumbling acrobats, strong men. They seemed to explode into the ring. There was so much happening, Tilly didn't know where to look.

The clowns were good. They ran into the audience and squirted people with water. Some of the acrobatics were

17

impressive too. But what Tilly really
wanted to see was the animals. The first
to perform were a team of dogs. They
reminded Tilly of her Jack Russell, Scruff,
only these ones were much more obedient.
They each wore a little red coat and hat,
which they didn't seem to mind at all.

'You should get Scruff an outfit like
that,' said Mia.

'He'd chew it to pieces in seconds,' said
Tilly, laughing.

The dogs took turns to complete an
assault course, which included
see-saws, podiums and
balance beams. The
finale was a series
of hoops that
got higher
and higher.

18

Eventually the dogs were practically flying to get through them. It looked very funny.

At the end of their performance the little dogs gathered round their trainer (who was dressed in a matching red coat and hat!) and jumped up at her enthusiastically as she praised them. It was clear to Tilly that these dogs were treated very well and loved their trainer. She wondered what would happen to them when the circus closed down.

There was no time to worry, however, because as soon as the dogs cleared the ring, a beautiful honey-coloured pony trotted out and showed himself off to the audience. Tilly's stomach filled with butterflies. She leaned forward in her seat.

'Introducing the fabulous Nimrod,' said the ringmaster. 'And his trainer, Clara Delfonte.'

Clara was a young girl, a few years older than Tilly and her friends. She was the most elegant person Tilly had ever seen. She wore a red-and-gold sequined leotard, and from head to toe, her skin sparkled, as though she'd been dipped in a pot of glitter. She followed Nimrod around the ring like a dainty fairy.

'I want to be *her*!' whispered Mia.

As the music grew faster, Clara hopped on to Nimrod's back and, rather than settle into position like Tilly would – sitting into the saddle, making sure she found her balance – Clara flicked her legs and did a handstand. She didn't wobble or shake.

As she did this, Nimrod broke into a fast trot.

Tilly and her friends stared in astonishment.

'How does she stay up like that?' said Cally.

'There must be wires,' said Tilly's dad.

'No wires,' said Duncan, who was sitting a few seats along. 'Just lots of practice.'

'And good horsemanship,' added Angela. 'Nimrod and Clara must have a very trusting, respectful relationship.'

With each lap, Nimrod got faster, but still Clara didn't wobble. She lifted one hand and balanced on the other. She did a somersault and landed on her feet. To finish, they jumped through a large silver hoop, then they did it again, this time with Nimrod jumping through it and Clara somersaulting over it, landing back in the saddle. Tilly was mesmerised.

She agreed with Angela. She knew from her own experience that a strong bond between a horse and its rider was a very special thing. Suddenly, she felt lucky that she had Magic Spirit and he had her. She couldn't imagine what she'd do without him. She knew she wasn't quite up to doing handstands on his back, but they definitely had lots of adventures ahead of them.

Tilly wondered if Clara felt the same about Nimrod. What was going to happen after tonight, when the circus closed for good? Were they going to be separated? It was too upsetting to think about.

When the show came to an end, everyone stood up and applauded. Because it was the last performance, as a treat, the ringmaster invited the audience into the ring to meet the performers. Tilly and her friends jumped at the chance. They headed straight towards Clara and Nimrod.

'He's beautiful,' said Tilly, admiring Nimrod's glossy coat and neat pale mane. 'How big is he? About 13hh?'

'13.2hh,' said Clara. 'Good guess.'

Tilly tried to call Angela over, to see if she could guess Nimrod's size too, but Angela was deep in conversation with the ringmaster, Mr Lyons.

'Aren't you scared?' said Mia, staring at the sequins on Clara's costume. 'When you're doing all that upside down, back-to-front stuff?'

'Never,' said Clara. 'Nimrod's a very intelligent pony. He senses every tiny movement I make and helps me keep my balance.'

Suddenly she sighed and closed her sparkly eyelids. 'I'm going to miss him so much.'

Nimrod lowered his head and looked sad.

'You mean you *are* going to be separated?' said Tilly, horrified. 'But you're so good together.'

'What will happen to you both?' asked Cally.

'I'm joining another circus troupe,' said Clara. 'We'll tour around Europe. It'll be really fun, but unfortunately Nimrod can't come with me. Mr Lyons will have to find him another home. Now that the circus is closing, he won't be able to keep any of the animals.'

Tilly reached up and tickled Nimrod's ears. She looked into his eyes. She could see he was smart and full of confidence.

But he was different to the other horses she knew, like Pride and Joy, Angela's event horse, or Red Admiral, the beautiful racehorse at Silver Shoe, who both had skill and determination in their blood. There was something mischievous about Nimrod, something that said 'I'm going to play a few tricks on you!'

Three

It was difficult getting up in the morning after such a late night. Nevertheless, Tilly had showered and dressed by the time the sun was rising. She pulled on an extra fleece to keep out the chilly winter wind and, with toast in one hand and a banana in the other, climbed into the back of her mum's car.

'How can you always be so chirpy at this hour?' said Tilly's mum.

This morning Tilly had good reason to

be chirpy. She was still thinking about the
circus performance.

'Did you see the way Clara Delfonte
did a handstand on Nimrod's back? How
does she balance like that? It was so cool.
I can't believe that's the last we'll see of
them.'

They pulled into the lane outside Silver
Shoe. The bare branches of the trees shook
in the wind. Tilly zipped up her fleece.

'Right, I'll pick you up later,' said her
mum. 'Don't go trying any handstands on
Magic, will you?'

'No, Mum.'

Magic was pleased when Tilly appeared at
the stable door. She was later than usual
and she could sense he was a bit anxious.

'Did you think I wasn't coming, boy?'
she said, stroking his neck and mane. 'Like
I wouldn't. You're my number one.'

She led him out to the yard and then began mucking out his stable. As she worked, she told him all about Clara and Nimrod and the closing circus.

'It's so sad, Magic. They won't get to perform together any more. I wish you could have seen Nimrod. He was such a clever pony. I know you would have liked him.'

Tilly unpacked Magic's grooming kit. She found a hoof pick and her best quality body brush.

'Let's get you smartened up. Your coat collects so much dirt in the winter.

All those muddy lanes and fields. Don't worry, by the time I'm finished you'll be gleaming!'

There were footsteps behind them.

'Morning, Tilly. Morning, Magic.'

Tilly looked up. It was Angela. She was standing beside Silver Shoe's only empty stable, holding a bucket of fresh water.

'Hi, Angela.'

'I heard you telling Magic about the circus. You really liked Nimrod, didn't you?'

'Yeah.'

'Me too.'

Angela gave a sheepish smile then disappeared inside the stable.

'What's she up to?' said Tilly thoughtfully.

Later that morning, Tilly and Mia were in the sand school, helping their friend Cynthia and her show pony Pickle train.

When Cynthia and Pickle had first come to Silver Shoe, Tilly had noticed they weren't bonding very well. Despite a few hiccups along the way, she'd encouraged them to have more fun together and now they were much happier.

Today they were trying a gymkhana game involving balloons and sticks. It was looking a bit messy but great fun at the same time!

'Um . . . keep trying,' said Mia. 'See how many you can catch.'

The balloons kept blowing away in the wind. Things weren't going to plan, but Cynthia was laughing and Pickle was cooperating with her, so that was a good sign.

After twenty minutes, they decided it was time to finish.

'Let's get some hot chocolate to warm us up,' said Mia.

'Good idea. I'm freezing,' said Cynthia.

She led Pickle down to the long field to graze with the other ponies, while Tilly and

Mia cleared up the equipment in the sand school. It was one of the Silver Shoe rules: always leave things tidy for other riders. When they were done, they headed for the club room.

As they turned into the yard an unexpected sight greeted them. Blocking the five-bar entrance gate, was the Lyons' Circus lorry. It seemed to be stuck, not quite in the yard and not quite out of it.

'Don't go any further,' said Angela's head boy, Duncan, as he directed the driver. 'It's too wide. You'll have to stop here.'

'Should be enough room for us to lead him out safely,' said Angela.

Tilly and Mia glanced at each other.

'Do you think this means . . . ?'

They both grinned.

'I knew Angela was up to something when I saw her earlier,' said Tilly. 'She must have been getting a stable ready.'

They watched as Clara Delfonte and the ringmaster, Mr Lyons, jumped out of the lorry cab and climbed into the back of the trailer. They came out moments later, leading Nimrod.

The girls couldn't contain their excitement. They ran towards Angela and Duncan.

'Is Nimrod really coming to stay at Silver Shoe?' said Mia.

'For a little while anyway,' said Angela. 'Just until Mr Lyons finds a permanent place for him.'

'Thank you so much,' said Clara. 'Even if it's only temporary, it feels good to know Nimrod is going to be well looked after when I go away.'

'You can be sure of that,' said Duncan. He ushered the girls forward. 'And with Tilly and Mia to help out, I expect he'll be spoilt rotten.'

'Oh, hi, girls,' said Clara. 'You were at the show last night, weren't you?'

'They're two of my best helpers,' said Angela.

Tilly beamed with pride. Clara smiled at her.

'Take great care of Nimrod. He's so special. He's very smart and quick to learn.

He loves to play. And, of course, he loves
to show off. I've worked with him for four
years and I've enjoyed every second of it.'

Clara reached up and gently stroked
Nimrod's cheek. Nimrod rested his head
on her shoulder. His expression was forlorn,
as though he knew they were going to be
parted. The sight made Tilly feel sad.

'Don't worry, Nimrod,' she said, trying
to make him feel better.
'We'll look after you.
You'll definitely
have a good
time at Silver
Shoe.'

'And feel free to visit whenever you get time off,' said Angela to Clara.

Clara nodded, tears glistening in her eyes.

Four

Once Clara and Mr Lyons had said their last goodbyes and carefully turned the lorry around, Angela suggested Tilly and Mia take Nimrod to see his stable.

'Come on,' said Tilly softly, as she started to lead Nimrod. 'Let's show you to your room. If you're only staying for a short while, I guess Silver Shoe will be like a hotel for you.'

Nimrod walked alongside the girls across the yard. The new surroundings seemed to be a good distraction from his sadness at saying goodbye to Clara, and he was soon sniffing around, trying to catch a glimpse of everything.

He was one of those ponies that could be described as 'bomb proof'. Everything was intriguing, rather than scary and alarming. Given his circus background, it was no surprise. He was probably used to all kinds of noise and action. Tilly thought he'd make a good riding school pony. Maybe she'd mention it to Angela.

'Here you go,' said Mia, opening the door to the stables. 'Chez Nimrod!'

But Nimrod was too busy checking out Mia's denim-look jodhpurs, which had sparkly stitching on them.

'He's a fashion victim!'

'Or maybe the sparkles remind him of all those sequins on Clara's leotard?' said Tilly.

'Of course!'

Mia moved closer so Nimrod could get a better look, and he nuzzled her cheek.

'It's obviously not just the sparkles he likes! Look how happy he seems with you,' said Tilly.

'Do you think so?' Mia looked pleased. 'Well, if he ever refuses to do something, we should remember he can be tempted with glitter!'

A few of the other Silver Shoe horses poked their heads over their stable doors, intrigued by the new guest.

'Time for a few introductions,' said
Tilly. 'Meet your neighbours. That's
Red Admiral – he's a super-fast racehorse.
And that's Lulabelle. She's the gentlest
mare you'll ever meet. I was there when
she gave birth to her foal, Lucky Chance.
It was magical. And over there, the
handsome grey, that's Magic Spirit.
He'll look after you.'

Angela had asked the girls to give Nimrod
some quiet time in his stable, so he could
get used to it. The bedding was already
prepared but there wasn't a hay-net.

'I'll go and fill one,' said Mia. 'You
lead him inside and get him settled.'

Tilly led Nimrod to the door and
allowed him to explore it. He seemed
particularly interested in the bolt, which
he tried to chew.

'It's to keep you safe,' Tilly explained.
'Look, you've got one of the nicest stables
on the block. It's really spacious.'

Nimrod stepped inside and stood back
against the wall. He walked forward and
poked his nose into each corner, as though
he was checking exactly how much space
he had. He didn't seem unsettled by the

new environment – it was as if he'd seen it all before. He was obviously used to travelling around a lot, but the stables at Silver Shoe clearly weren't nearly as exciting as the colourful circus trailers.

Nimrod rubbed his back against a wooden beam, then scraped his hoof against the wall panel.

'Hmm, you don't seem overly impressed,' said Tilly. 'I'm afraid it's not quite as fun as backstage at the circus, but you'll get used to it.'

Nimrod gave her an inquisitive look. His eyes flashed with intelligence.

'I expect you'll get up to a few tricks while you're here, won't you?'

Tilly could tell by the way his ears pricked up that he was already planning something. He lifted his head and snorted.

'Thought so.'

Mia returned with the hay-net. She tied it safely to a ring on the wall, and made sure it was high enough that Nimrod wouldn't get his feet caught in it. Then she

42

and Tilly sat with their backs against the stable door.

'I can't wait for a ride,' said Mia, admiring Nimrod's delicate build. He wasn't big, like Pride and Joy, or Magic. He was petite and lithe, like a gymnast, like his old partner, Clara.

'I bet he likes lots of exercise,' said Tilly. 'I'm sure Angela would be keen for you to work together. It's a shame he's so small, otherwise you two would make a good match.'

'If only I could say that about the horses I've been looking at recently,' said Mia. 'My parents are getting tired of driving round the country trying to find the right horse for me. They think I'm too fussy. But it's got to feel right. Like you and Magic. I want my new horse to be special, at least as wonderful as Rosie. Sometimes I wonder if it's ever going to happen. Am I doing something wrong?'

Mia, Cally, and Tilly had all shared Rosie between them at one time, and she'd

43

always have a place in their hearts. Tilly
did most of her riding on Magic Spirit now,
which Angela and Duncan were grateful
for. Magic had a tendency to be tricky
for other riders, but for Tilly, he always
behaved. Cally had her own horse, Mr
Fudge, who was stabled at Cavendish Hall
boarding school. Now it was Mia's turn.

'You'll get there,' said Tilly. 'You just
have to be patient. You'll find the right one
eventually.'

'I hope so,' said Mia. There was
disappointment in her voice. 'None of
the ones I've seen so far have been right.
They're either too big and bulky, or they're
quiet and dozy, or they don't like this and
that and the other. I don't want a fussy
ride. I want one with spirit, one that's a bit
cheeky, one that likes to explore and be
playful.'

'Like you, you mean.'

Mia smiled.

Tilly didn't say anything more, but as
she looked at Nimrod, she remembered
how he'd reacted to Mia earlier. As a little
circus pony, she knew Nimrod was too
small for Mia to ride regularly, but he had
everything she'd just mentioned. Spirit,
cheek and playfulness. Maybe getting to
know Nimrod would help Mia realise that
it was possible for her to have a special
relationship with another horse. He might
help her get her confidence back.

'We'd better get going,' said Mia,
looking at her watch. 'We told Cynthia

45

we'd meet her in the club room for hot
chocolate.'

'Oops!' said Tilly. 'I'd completely
forgotten about that! We'd better go –
quick.'

They got to their feet and said goodbye.

'See you later then, boy,' said Mia.
'Good to have you here!'

Five

As they walked over to the club room,
Tilly's mobile buzzed.

'It's Brook,' she said, answering the
call.

Brook was Tilly's older brother. They
had been adopted at birth and raised by
different families. They'd discovered
they were brother and sister thanks to the
unusual matching horsehair bracelets they
both wore, given to them by their real mum
before she died.

Even though Tilly and Brook had been separated for most of their lives, they were united by a love of horses. If anyone understood Tilly's relationship with Magic Spirit, it was Brook. He had a wonderful horse of his own, called Solo, and was a promising young rider.

'Hello,' she said.

'Hey, Tilly!'

'Any reply yet?'

Tilly was eager to hear if there had been a response to the letter she and Brook had sent to the chief of a Native American tribe, who wore horsehair bracelets like their own. They wanted to know if there was any connection between this tribe and their mum. Neither Tilly nor Brook remembered anything about her, but now they'd found each other they were on a mission to find out more about their real family.

'No. Nothing.'

'Oh.'

They'd sent the letter months ago.

'Don't worry. I'm sure we'll hear something soon.'

'I hope so,' said Tilly anxiously. She couldn't bear the waiting. She was beginning to lose hope.

'I was calling to see if you guys fancied meeting for a hack after school tomorrow,' said Brook. 'The weather forecast is good.'

Tilly looked at Mia and made a riding gesture with her hands. Mia nodded.

'Definitely. Meet you outside the gates of Cavendish Hall, as usual?'

'Great. See you then.'

Tilly and Mia regularly met Brook and Cally at Cavendish Hall. The surrounding grounds were great for hacks, with long woody tracks well away from the road.

'Excellent,' said Mia. Then she sighed. 'But which horse can I take? Rosie has a lesson after school tomorrow, and I'm always borrowing other people's horses.'

'You're good with Watson,' said Tilly. 'And he'd love the exercise.'

'I suppose so,' said Mia. 'But I wish I

could find the perfect horse of my own.
I just don't know what kind of horse I'm
looking for.'

'Isn't it obvious?' said Tilly. 'Begins with
a 'Nim' and ends with a 'rod'? You want a
horse like him.'

'Nimrod? Really? Do you think he's got
the right kind of personality for me?'

Her eyes lit up. Tilly wondered why it
was sometimes so hard to see the things
that were right in front of you.

By the time Tilly and Mia reached the
club room, Cynthia was sitting with
three hot chocolates, looking bored. The
marshmallows, which were supposed to be
floating on the top, had completely melted.

'I thought you were never coming,' she
moaned.

'Sorry,' said Mia. 'We got side-tracked.
Tilly had a call from Brook. And before

that, we had to help Angela and Duncan
with the new pony.'

'I saw the lorry arrive.'

'Yes, his name's Nimrod. Angela's doing
a favour for the owner of Lyons' Circus by
looking after him for a while. Did you see
him? He's gorgeous.'

'We had to put him in his stable,' said
Tilly.

'And get him settled.'

'Well, you didn't do a very good job,'
said Cynthia, as she peered out of the
window. 'Look.'

To Tilly's surprise, there was Nimrod,
out in the yard, munching on Jack Fisher's
plants. He wasn't tied and there was no one
supervising him.

'He shouldn't be doing that!'

'Who let him out?' exclaimed Tilly.

'We bolted the stable door . . . didn't
we?'

But there was no time to worry now. A
loose pony in a yard could be dangerous.
There were all sorts of hazards – reversing

vehicles, stable equipment, or even other horses. There was also the risk of Nimrod escaping, not to mention the fact that Jack Fisher wouldn't be happy if his entire plant collection was eaten!

The girls ran outside.

'You go first, Tilly,' said Mia, keeping her voice low. 'You're best in a horse crisis!'

'No, you go,' said Tilly. 'He really seemed to like you just now.'

Mia slowed to a walk. She got close to Nimrod and quietly took hold of his head collar. He pulled away at first, but Mia made a calming noise to reassure him. Moments later, Duncan wandered out of the tack room. As soon as he realised what was going on, he came to help. Together, he, Mia and Tilly led Nimrod back to his stable.

'It's lucky we caught him before the yard got busy. Anything could have happened. It's not like you to forget to bolt a door, Tilly,' he said.

He didn't sound cross but there was a serious tone to his voice. It made Tilly feel bad.

'But I did. I did bolt the door. I'm certain. At least I think I am. But, oh, I'm sorry, Duncan.'

'It's okay. These things happen. But

you'll remember to double check next time, won't you?'

'Absolutely.'

Six

Tilly *had* bolted the stable door. She was
sure of it. Then again, she and Mia had
been in a hurry to meet Cynthia. Maybe
in the rush she hadn't done it properly. She
was cross with herself for being so careless.
She hated the idea that she might have
put a horse in danger. She was also worried
Duncan and Angela would stop trusting
her.

Alone, she walked down to the bottom
field to check on Magic. She knew he'd

make her feel better. He was there, munching grass, alongside Pickle, Red Admiral and Lucky Chance. As soon as Magic saw her, he came to the fence.

'Hello, boy,' she said.

He nuzzled into her shoulder and sniffed her face.

'I really hope it wasn't my fault,' she whispered, as she closed her eyes and let the whiskers of Magic's muzzle tickle her skin. She didn't need to explain. Magic seemed to understand. He nudged the side of her chin with his nose, as though he was trying to make her smile.

It wasn't long before Lucky Chance joined them, keen to get some fuss and attention. Tilly remembered the day Lucky had been born. She was so much bigger now, but she still looked youthful and dainty next to Magic and Red. It was great to see her hanging out with the big boys! It wouldn't be long before her training began. She was already used to a halter and she was happy to stand tied in the

yard, or to be touched all over, which was
important when it came to good grooming
habits. Tilly hoped she could help out with
Lucky's training. It fascinated her to see
how horses could learn, and how they could
be taught.

'You'll do well, won't you, Lucky?' she
said, tickling the tuft of mane between
Lucky's ears. 'I bet you're really clever.
And there are plenty of other clever

horses around Silver Shoe to inspire you. Red with his racing talent. Rosie with her lovely, gentle temperament. Pride with his eventing skills. Magic with his all round wonderfulness.'

Magic pricked his ears.

'Oh, and I mustn't forget our very clever guest pony, Nimrod. I expect he could show you a trick or two.'

Feeling better, Tilly returned to the yard, but as she came through the shortcut between the barns, an unexpected sight greeted her. It was Nimrod!

Tilly blinked. 'Are you supposed to be here?'

There was no one with him. He stood, swishing his tail and looking ever so pleased with himself. Puzzled, Tilly took hold of his halter and led him back to the yard. The first thing she noticed was that Nimrod's stable door was open again. Duncan was standing in front of it, looking panicked.

'Oh! Thank goodness. Where did you find him?'

'Um, he was trying to get through the shortcut to the fields.'

'I thought I'd shut him in. I turned my back for a second and – wait a minute – I think I know what's going on here. I heard about a pony who could do this once . . . '

Duncan took Nimrod from Tilly and led him back to his stable.

'Watch this,' he said, beckoning Tilly over.

He closed the bottom half of the stable door, pulled the bolt, checked it was firmly in place, then stood back. Sure enough, Nimrod leaned his head over and with a few deft moves worked his teeth and muzzle round the bolt. Within seconds, the door was open and he was making another bid for freedom.

'Whoa!' said Tilly. She didn't know whether to be impressed or alarmed.

'At least this clears our names,' said Duncan, stopping Nimrod in his tracks.

'Clara warned us he knew a few tricks.
Looks like opening doors is one of them.
I think I'll have to put an extra catch on the
door. One that's Nimrod-proof!'

Nimrod shook his mane then pulled
back his lips, as though he was laughing.

'You're a cheeky one all right!'

'I wonder what other tricks he knows,'
said Tilly.

'I'm sure we'll find out,' said Duncan.
'One thing's for certain though, smart
ponies like Nimrod need to be kept
busy. They need lots of stimulation and
challenge, otherwise they get bored. And
when they're bored, they get mischievous.
Perhaps you and Mia can help out?'

'How?'

'I noticed Mia's taken a real shine to
Nimrod. I know she's feeling low about
not having her own horse at the moment
– he might take her mind off it. And I can
always trust you to solve a horse problem,
Tilly. The pair of you can keep him out
of trouble, make sure he's occupied and

having fun. Keep an eye on him around the farm, that sort of thing.'

'Sure,' said Tilly. She was pleased Duncan had used the word 'trust'. 'I'll suggest it to Mia right away. But I know she'll say yes. She and Nimrod seem like two of a kind.'

Duncan laughed. 'Maybe they are.'

Seven

As Tilly predicted, Mia was delighted to help out with Nimrod.

'We'll start after school tomorrow,' she said. 'I'll see if Angela will let me ride him over to Cavendish Hall to meet the others.'

'Good plan.'

The next day seemed to drag on forever. Tilly found it hard to concentrate on her school work. She was constantly thinking about escaping ponies and tricks. She also hoped Brook might have some news about their letter. It was nerve-wracking just thinking about it.

When the last bell finally went, Tilly raced to meet Mia at the gates where Mia's mum was waiting for them. She always took the girls to Silver Shoe after school. Mia's mum was a hairdresser and every week she had a different style. Today it was a plum-coloured spiky crop.

'Nice,' said Tilly. 'I like it!'

Tilly was relieved to notice Duncan had fixed a strong latch to the bottom of Nimrod's stable door. He couldn't reach it now, even with his nimble teeth. The girls went to the tack room to change into their stable clothes and collect their grooming kits, then they got straight to work.

They groomed Magic and Nimrod side by side in the yard. Tilly didn't want Magic to feel left out, but she couldn't help

peeking over and admiring Nimrod's lovely coat. It was in very good condition.

'Can we swap for a bit?' she said, keen to get a closer look at him.

'Sure.'

Mia took Magic's body brush from Tilly and went towards him. Magic raised his nose in the air and looked away disapprovingly.

'Hey fella, don't be jealous,' she said. 'Your favourite girl is hanging out with Nimrod for a bit. But she'll come straight back to you, don't worry.'

Tilly, meanwhile, took a comb to Nimrod's mane and tail. His fair hair was beautifully soft and creamy coloured, and he seemed to love the attention. No wonder Clara hadn't wanted to say goodbye. Tilly couldn't resist gathering up the stray strands and putting them in her pocket. She wondered if Angela had contact details for Clara's new circus troupe.

Tilly and Mia tacked up and began their journey through the quiet lanes.

When they reached Cavendish Hall, Brook and Cally were waiting for them at the gates. Tilly couldn't wait to ask.

'Anything in the post yet? Any reply?'

Brook shook his head.

'Sorry.'

'I thought there'd be something by now. Maybe our letter hasn't reached them. Should we send another one?'

'Let's give it another week,' said Brook, 'then we'll think about a plan B.'

'What's plan B?'

Brook shrugged.

It was very frustrating. Tilly wanted an answer, even if it was a, 'No, we haven't had anything to do with your mum.' She adjusted her horsehair bracelets, the one from Magic's tail and the one her real mum had given her when she was born, and tried to put it out of her mind.

'Let's get hacking,' said Mia. 'Not long until it gets dark.'

The air was chilly and the sun was already low, spreading a soft pink light across the sky, which looked lovely against the orange and red of the tree tops. Luckily everyone had remembered their high visibility tabards.

'What a striking pony,' said Brook, as they walked out together.

'Meet Nimrod. Circus pony and top trickster!'

'He's an escapologist,' said Tilly.

'He's a what?' said Cally.

Tilly and Mia explained the story of Nimrod's door-opening habit, to Cally and Brook's amazement. They came out on to a wide forest track with lovely sandy ground and began to trot. Angela had warned them never to trot or canter on the rougher, stonier paths.

'If he's worked in a circus all his life,' said Brook, admiring Nimrod's athletic top line, 'he must be very agile.'

As though keen to prove himself, Nimrod suddenly advanced towards a fallen log.

'Hey! Easy, boy,' Mia called, trying to stop him.

To everyone's surprise, Nimrod lifted
his front hooves on to the log, then
manoeuvred to the side and lifted his back
hooves, until he was perched on top. He
looked at the other horses, as if to say, 'Ha!
I'm so clever!'

Mia clung on tightly, because even though Nimrod was steady, she was wobbling all over the place.

'Whoa! I don't think I'm quite up to Clara Delfonte's acrobatic standards!'

Eventually they stepped down on the other side, with Mia smiling, looking relieved and proud to still be in the saddle.

'Well I thought Solo was talented, but there's no way he could do anything like that,' said Brook. 'He's so big, he'd probably flatten that log!'

'Nor Mr Fudge,' said Cally. 'But it's okay, boy, I love you anyway.' She patted Mr Fudge reassuringly.

'What about Magic?' said Mia. 'Do you reckon he's got the agility?'

Tilly nodded. 'I'm not sure about the balancing. I think it's wiser to leave that to trained circus ponies, but we have been working on something ... come on, boy,' she whispered. 'Show them what you can do!'

She nudged Magic forward, and he picked up a relaxed canter. Tilly guided him towards the log, then sat up and kept her balance as Magic leapt over the log, with plenty of height and style.

When Tilly turned to see her friends' reactions, they were staring at her with open mouths.

'Wow! That was a jump and a half!' said Cally.

'Where did that come from?' said Mia.

'You two looked like a professional cross-country partnership,' said Brook. 'You and Magic have really come on.'

Tilly blushed. She had to admit, she hadn't quite expected it to be so good herself. She leaned forward and whispered in Magic's ear.

'Good boy. You certainly showed them. If balancing on logs isn't your thing, jumping them clearly is!'

Eight

Next day, after school, Tilly and Mia were surprised to find Tilly's mum picking them up, rather than Mia's mum.

'She called to say she's running late,' Mrs Redbrow explained. 'She's busy organising a hairstyling competition at the college, so I'm taking you to Silver Shoe today. Adam has just finished football practice so he and Scruff are coming too.'

Tilly peered into the back of the car. Scruff was wagging his tail and Adam,

dressed in muddy football kit, was pulling faces at her.

'My charming younger brother!' she said to Mia, rolling her eyes.

They climbed into the car and Scruff started yapping. Tilly cuddled him.

'He gets as excited to see you as Magic does,' said Mia. 'Almost.'

The car pulled away from the school gates and the girls began discussing other kinds of tricks they thought Nimrod might be able to do.

'Well, we know he can balance. And open doors. Do you reckon he can grip a brush in his teeth and comb another horse's tail?'

Tilly laughed. 'That's bonkers, Mia. But I bet he can.'

'You think your pony is so clever,' said Adam. 'But can he do this?'

He held his football and tried to spin it on his fingertip. It worked for a second then rolled on to his lap.

'Oh, wow! That's mind-blowing!' said

Mia sarcastically.

Adam tutted. 'You two don't know anything. Football is way better than horses.'

'Yeah, right.'

When they arrived at the farm, the girls took Scruff for a run around the grounds while Tilly's mum chatted with Angela. Adam found a quiet area beside the long field, where he could practise his ball skills.

'Watch where that ball goes,' warned Tilly. 'Don't frighten the horses with it.'

Scruff was delighted to be free. He stuck his nose in every open door and into every corner, excitedly looking for mice. The horses didn't frighten him

and he didn't frighten them. Some were inquisitive, but never scared.

Eventually, Tilly picked him up.

'Right. We'd better get on with our duties. Scruff, you go and play with Adam for a bit. You can keep each other out of mischief.'

She set him off in the direction of the long field, then she and Mia made their way to the tack room. Tilly pulled on her favourite pair of jodhpurs, which were getting quite tatty, but were too comfy to throw away. Mia had a black pair and an old Pony Club camp t-shirt.

They left the tack room, with their grooming kits in hand, and went to find Magic and Nimrod.

'Magic must be grazing,' said Tilly, peering into his empty stable.

'Nimrod too.'

Angela saw the girls and broke away from her conversation with Tilly's mum to point them in the direction of the long field.

'Uh oh,' said Tilly. 'That's where Adam went with his football. I hope he hasn't been kicking it at them.'

'He wouldn't do that, would he?'

'Not intentionally. But his ball control isn't as good as he claims it is. Believe me, the number of windows he's smashed . . . '

With that, the girls quickened their pace, worried they would find a bunch of terrified horses cowering together, trying to dodge a mis-aimed football.

'I can hear something,' said Mia, straining to listen. It was the sound of Scruff yapping. And Adam yelling.

'Oh, no!'

As they ran around the corner, expecting the worst, their mouths dropped open. Something amazing was happening. They stopped and watched.

Adam was kicking the ball over the fence, as far across the field as he could, then Nimrod was galloping forwards and nudging it back with his nose and hooves.

77

'There you go!' cried Adam. 'A footballing pony! I take back what I said earlier. How cool is that?'

'Agreed,' said Mia, wide-eyed. 'That. Is. Cool.'

As the ball rolled along, Nimrod followed it. When Scruff dived in and

tried to tackle it away, Nimrod stamped his hoof. Scruff yapped and retreated.

'Clever Nimrod,' said Tilly. 'But don't be a ball-hogger!'

'How did you know Nimrod could do that?' Mia asked Adam.

'He just did it. As soon as he saw me with the ball, he came over and tried to get through the gate. He was chewing at the latch and everything.'

Tilly and Mia glanced at each other.

'I figured it was the ball he was after, so I showed it to him, and he immediately knocked it out of my hand with his nose. That's when he started dribbling with it. I like this pony!'

Adam held the ball in his arms and Nimrod came to the fence. Tilly and Mia patted and praised him.

'You're one of the smartest ponies I know,' said Tilly. 'If you could pass your footballing skills on to some of the other Silver Shoe horses, we'd have a whole team!'

'Nimrod! We belong together, you and me. I wish you could stay at Silver Shoe forever,' said Mia. 'We're two of a kind.'

'In your dreams,' muttered Adam, giving Mia one of his cheekiest grins.

It wasn't long before Magic also appeared at the fence. He stood next to Nimrod and tried to push him to the side with his hind quarters.

'I think he's jealous,' said Mia.

'Oh, Magic,' said Tilly, reaching up to stroke his nose. 'You're smart too. You're the only horse for me. Don't you worry about that.'

Magic lowered his head, soothed by Tilly's affection.

'You don't need to play football to be wonderful,' she whispered. Then to the others, she said, 'It would be fun, though, wouldn't it? If we could get some of the other horses involved in Nimrod's football trick?'

'They could play a match,' suggested Mia.

'We could film it and make a video,' said Adam. 'We could call it 'Match of the Hay'!'

He laughed. Tilly and Mia groaned.

'Stick to football, eh?' said Mia. 'Leave the comedy to the experts,' she added, pointing at herself.

Nine

For the next few days, alongside their daily
riding the girls got Nimrod to practise
his football tricks. Mia was determined
to develop his skill and, with Tilly's help,
they took a ball down to the long field and
encouraged Nimrod to nudge, kick or roll
it back to them. It caused quite a stir
around the farm, and a few of the Silver
Shoe riders came to watch.

On the third day, Nimrod was really
getting the idea that when Mia or Tilly

rolled the ball towards him, he had to pass it back. He was eager to keep doing it and happy to go for longer distances.

'I think the world deserves to see this,' said Mia. 'We should put on a Nimrod show.'

'I've got an idea,' said Duncan, who'd been admiring the action from the fence. 'What about having a display in the sand school and inviting everyone from Silver Shoe? We could do it next Saturday. Make an event of it and raise some money for charity.'

'We could donate the money to World Horse Welfare,' suggested Tilly. 'And get some of the other horses to join in, doing their own displays.'

'Good idea!'

With no time to lose, the girls set to work practising a range of displays with the other horses and ponies.

Duncan was going to do some rodeo riding on Red Admiral. Tilly and Angela were going to give a demonstration on Magic Spirit and Pride and Joy going over narrow skinny arrowhead jumps and lots of angled rails, and Cynthia was planning to show off Parkview Pickle's gymkhana skills.

Then, as the last show before Nimrod's grand finale, Duncan suggested it might be fun to show off the girls' skills on a lunge, without stirrups or reins. They did this exercise fairly regularly, because Angela said it was a great way to help riders find their balance without leaning on their hands. Angela stood in the middle holding Rosie's lunge rein as, one after another, Tilly, Mia and Cynthia performed various exercises, like circling their arms, or touching their toes. Rosie seemed to love every second of it, and performed like a dream. And as Mia pointed out, another horse might have bucked her clean off when she badly lost her balance and ended up clutching around Rosie's neck!

The rehearsals seemed to go well, and when all the plans were finalised, Duncan made flyers to advertise the display. The three girls sat up on the fence, admiring his handiwork.

'So, Pickle's got the gig,' said Mia, talking like a show director. 'She'll be one of our star performers. And Pride and Joy too. He's got the instinct for showing off.'

'And Magic,' said Tilly.

'That goes without saying, of course. One nudge from you and he does whatever he's asked. He's definitely in!'

When Saturday came around, the weather was perfect. It was cold, but the sky was clear and the sun was bright. A large crowd gathered at the perimeter of the sand school. Most of the Silver Shoe regulars were there, as well as Tilly and Mia's parents.

Tilly and Mia stood with Magic and Nimrod and watched from a distance. Tilly kept her hands busy, plaiting the hairs from Nimrod's tail to make a bracelet. She'd intended to

give it to Clara, but now she wondered
whether she should give it to Mia instead.
Tilly had made bracelets for lots of people,
but still not Mia, and she definitely
deserved one.

'All these people,' said Mia, staring at
the crowds. 'It's making me nervous.'

'Oh, don't worry,' said Tilly. 'This is all
about fun. Let's just enjoy it.'

They could see Angela bobbing through
the crowd. She'd made a large pot of soup
and was passing it round to the onlookers.
She came over to Tilly and Mia and gave
them each a serving.

'Drink up,' she said. 'It's my special
homemade mushroom soup. It'll give you
fuel and warm you up.'

Magic peered over her shoulder and
tried to get a taste of it himself.

'Hey, it's a bit hot for you! Well done,
girls. You've gathered quite a crowd. Let's
hope we raise lots of money. I hope you
don't mind, but I've invited some special
guests. They're not here yet, but fingers

crossed they'll arrive in time to see the action.'

'Who?'

'You'll see.'

With that, she disappeared with her pot of soup.

Mia looked at Tilly.

'Who does she mean?'

'I don't know.'

'What about Brook and Cally?' said Mia. 'Aren't they supposed to be coming too?'

'They're riding over from Cavendish Hall,' said Tilly, glancing at her watch. 'I hope they're not late.'

'Perfect timing!'

Tilly looked up. Brook and Cally had just arrived and were tying their horses, Solo and Mr Fudge, on the other side of the yard.

'Go and say hi,' said Mia. 'I'll watch Magic for you.'

Tilly started to make her way over, and as she got close, she saw Brook running towards her. He was waving something in his hand. Instantly, Tilly had a feeling it was what she hoped it would be. Her stomach did a somersault.

'We've got it!' cried Brook. 'The letter! They've replied!'

'Show me! Show me!'

Brook held it out. It was a small white rectangular envelope, like any other, but it had an airmail sticker and beautiful golden eagle stamp in the corner.

'I haven't opened it yet. I thought we should read it together.'

'Hey, you two,' said Cally. 'I'll go and find Mia and let you look at the letter in peace.'

Tilly stared at the envelope. Suddenly it seemed like the whole world was spinning. This little envelope, she realised, might tell them everything they wanted to know.

'Well, open it then!'

Brook slid his finger beneath the flap and carefully eased it along the seal. He took out the sheet of paper inside.

Dear Brook and Tilly,

Thank you for your letter. I'm sorry it has taken so long for a reply, but I wanted to wait till one of our elders, Running River, came back from his wilderness retreat. He has a great memory for faces and I thought he would know best of all if your mother had spent any time with us. We showed him the photo and told him about your horsehair bracelets, which do, indeed, look similar to the bracelets traditionally worn by members of our tribe. Running River thought about it for a long time, then he told me the woman in the photograph was familiar to him. We have lots of people coming and going at

our reserve, but he is certain she was one of them. She went by the name of Sweet Rose. He remembers her because of her English accent. That's all he can recall for now, but if you have any further questions or want to find out more about our tribe do not hesitate to contact me. Email might be quicker – 4paws@gmail.com

Kind regards,

Chief Four Paws

Ten

'Tilly. C'mon. Everyone's waiting for you,' called Mia.

Tilly looked at Brook, then back at the letter. Her heart was pounding.

'This is great. It must be her. Don't you think so?'

'Sounds like a strong possibility,' he replied, smiling.

'Tilly! It's time!' called Mia again.

'I'd better go,' said Tilly. 'Let's look at it again later.'

She sprinted back to the stables, where Mia and Magic were waiting. She felt light and happy, as though she was starting to make sense of things. It was like putting together the pieces of a very important jigsaw puzzle.

Magic was tacked up, so all she had to do was mount and follow the others into the sand school. She couldn't resist quickly telling him about the letter though. He was always the first to know what was going on in Tilly's life.

'Right. Let's go and show off our skills,' she said, patting him on the neck.

Each horse took their turn with their rider. Duncan went first with Red Admiral and did some fantastic rodeo style riding, hurling a lasso over a fence-post. Everyone whooped and cheered. Tilly couldn't help noticing Angela admiring him in his cowboy hat and chaps.

When the cheering stopped, Cynthia followed on Pickle.

Then it was Angela and Tilly's turn.

Their act went very smoothly, and Tilly was delighted at Magic's performance in front of his first audience.

The lunge lessons went well too, but the girls had fits of laughter when poor Mia lost her balance once again and had to grab hold of Rosie's neck to stay on.

At last, it was Nimrod's turn to
demonstrate his talent for football. For
some reason, today he didn't seem as
engaged, or as enthusiastic as he had done
earlier in the week. Mia rolled the ball
towards him, but he just looked at it.

'What's up? You were so keen the other day,' she whispered. 'Look! A ball! Remember how you went after the ball?'

Nimrod lifted his head. He shook his mane then stopped. He took a few steps back, as though he was doing a double take. Tilly watched from the fence as Mia struggled to entice him with the ball. She wondered what had caught his attention, then she noticed two familiar faces in the crowd. It was Mr Lyons and Clara Delfonte. They must be Angela's special guests!

It was obvious to Tilly that Nimrod had spotted them too. He immediately lowered his head and began doing what Mia had wanted him to do all along. He rolled the ball, nudging it with his nose, managing a full circuit of the sand school, past Red and Pickle, past Magic. The crowd cheered wildly. After all the waiting, they were delighted.

Tilly could see a huge grin on Mia's face and she was pleased for her. She didn't

mind that she
and Magic
weren't the
biggest stars
of the day.
She already
felt good from
head to toe
because of her
letter.

'We'll leave
football to Nimrod, hey?' she whispered,
as she tickled Magic's ears.

When Clara came over, Tilly saw Nimrod
quiver with joy. He pricked his ears forward
and stepped towards her. She greeted him
with cuddles and kisses.

'I'm impressed,' she said. 'Nice trick.
You've obviously kept him busy.'

'Thanks,' said Mia.

'I thought you'd gone abroad with your new circus,' said Tilly.

'Yes, I flew in from Croatia this morning. We've just finished rehearsals and I've got a week off before the show starts properly. I wanted to see how Nimrod was getting on, so I booked a flight.'

'I understand,' said Tilly. She looked over at Magic and knew she'd do the same. And she knew exactly what to do with the horsehair bracelet she'd made too. She pulled it out of her pocket.

'Here, I made you this, to remember him by. It's from his tail-hairs.'

'Oh,' said Clara, sniffing. 'That's so nice, I'm going to cry. I miss Nimrod so much, I'll treasure this. Thank you so much, Tilly. He's a great pony.'

'We think he's great too,' said Mia. 'He's fitted in really well at Silver Shoe. I wish he could stay.'

'Well,' said Clara. 'Funny you should say that. Mr Lyons is having a word with Angela. We've seen how settled Nimrod is here.

We think it would be a good permanent home, if there's any way it could be arranged.'

Mia's eyes nearly bulged out of her head.

'Wow, we'd be happy to look after him!'

Moments later, Mr Lyons and Angela appeared. They were smiling, which looked like a good sign. Tilly couldn't help feeling a bit nervous though. She knew Mia had bonded with Nimrod, and even if he was too small for her to be able to ride regularly, at least he'd shown Mia that finding the right horse wasn't impossible. And until she found her perfect horse, Nimrod might be the ideal choice.

'Great news,' said Angela.

Tilly sighed with relief.

'Nimrod will be staying at Silver Shoe as a riding school pony. He's good-natured and responsive – it looks like he might be with us for a long while.'

Tilly and Mia cheered and clapped hands, then hugged each other.

'Well, that went down well,' said Mr Lyons.

'It couldn't be better,' said Mia. She reached up and stroked Nimrod's face. Although he was standing close to Clara, he responded straightaway to the gesture.

'I can tell he likes you,' said Clara. She
patted Nimrod's neck. 'I guess it's over to
you from now on.'

Mia gulped. 'Thank you. We'll take care
of him, I promise.'

'I know you will,' said Clara.

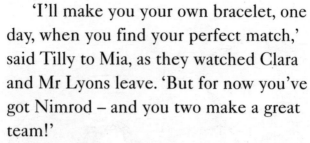

'I'll make you your own bracelet, one day, when you find your perfect match,' said Tilly to Mia, as they watched Clara and Mr Lyons leave. 'But for now you've got Nimrod – and you two make a great team!'

Mia smiled, and Tilly was glad. She couldn't wait for all of them to go riding together, and for all the adventures they were going to have. Then she looked into Magic's eyes and stroked his cheek.

'Mia and Nimrod aren't the only great team,' she whispered.

And, as if in total agreement, Magic nodded.

Pippa's Top Tips

Even if you ride the same tracks regularly, always be aware of your surroundings – a new signpost or a fallen tree could easily spook your horse or pony.

During the winter, your horse's coat will collect much more dirt, so make sure you give them a thorough groom after those muddy hacks!

Always tie your horse's hay-net safely to the ring on the wall. It should be high enough to ensure your horse's feet won't get caught in it, and tied with a special safety knot.

Always make sure the stable door is properly shut, and have a bottom bolt – especially for the escape artists!

A loose pony in a yard can be very dangerous. There are all sorts of dangers – reversing vehicles, stable equipment, even other horses.

If you have a pony that can undo a bolt, use a lead rope and clip it to the door as extra security, and if they're turned out, make sure all gates are securely shut!

Regularly check the fencing around field to ensure your horse is secure. If the fence is wire, take extra care, because your horse could easily injure himself on it.

If the tracks you usually ride down are very stony and uneven, try and stay in walk. If you have to trot, keep your eyes down and pick the best bit of ground.

If you're hacking and you spot an open gate, or if you need to go through a gate that's closed, always shut it behind you.

Lunging a horse without stirrups or reins is a great way to help riders find their balance without leaning on their hands. But make sure you do it on a very safe pony or horse, and have someone experienced lunging you who can help you with your position.

For more about Tilly and Silver Shoe Farm –
including pony tips, quizzes and everything
you ever wanted to know about horses –
visit www.tillysponytails.co.uk